Ethelbert Dudley Warfield

Joseph Cabell Breckinridge, Junior

Ensign in the United States Navy

Ethelbert Dudley Warfield

Joseph Cabell Breckinridge, Junior
Ensign in the United States Navy

ISBN/EAN: 9783744747790

Printed in Europe, USA, Canada, Australia, Japan

Cover: Foto ©Raphael Reischuk / pixelio.de

More available books at **www.hansebooks.com**

Joseph Cabell Breckinridge, Junior

ENSIGN IN THE UNITED STATES NAVY

A BRIEF STORY OF A SHORT LIFE

The noblest men methinks are bred
Of ours the Saxo-Norman race."
TENNYSON.

BY

ETHELBERT DUDLEY WARFIELD

PRESIDENT OF LAFAYETTE COLLEGE

The Knickerbocker Press
New York
1898

CONTENTS

APPENDICES

iii

INTRODUCTION

" Leaves have their time to fall,
And flowers to wither at the north wind's breath,
And stars to set ;—but all,
Thou hast all seasons for thy own, O Death."
—Hemans.

T HE completeness of a human life is not to be measured by its length, nor even by its accomplishment, but rather by what it represents. Some lives are beautiful because of their symmetrical development, growing step by step, unfolding from bud to blossom, and blossom to fruit, until perfect maturity is attained. Other lives are beautiful because of their striking vi

incompleteness of development, because they have given all the beauty
and strength which they possessed
for the accomplishment of a single
noble act in the service of a beloved
cause, or in a sudden passion of sub-
lime self-sacrifice. The world has
always yearned over the unfulfilled
promise of these brief lives, and con-
tinues to study with never-ceasing
regret the lives of the Stephens, and
Sydneys, and Warrens, of history.
The poets are in their tenderest
moods when they sing of them, as
Milton, and Shelley, and Tennyson
sing in their *Lycidas*, *Adonais*, and
In Memoriam. This impulse must
be the excuse for this brief sketch of
one whose life was so short, and
whose death, dignified as it was by
devotion to duty, was yet but one of
the passing incidents of the unselfish
service to which he had dedicated
his young manhood.

Joseph Cabell Breckinridge lost his

life in what may be regarded as
the first episode in our war with
Spain. He was swept overboard
from the torpedo - boat *Cushing*,
while it was bearing despatches to
the *Maine*, then lying in the harbor
of Havana. The news of the destruction of the *Maine* reached New
York while the writer of this memoir
was waiting to receive the body of
the young sailor which the steamship *Seneca* was bringing home. An
additional incident is added to this
first page of war history, by the death
of Ensign Breckinridge's close friend
and classmate, Ensign Worth Bag-
ley, who was the first officer to be
killed in an actual engagement. The
progress of the war has been so rapid,
so many have proved themselves
worthy of the name of hero, so superb is the record of our army and
navy, that the story of this brief
life may seem to some insignificant.
But that is precisely what it is not.

It is significant of the honorable fact, that not only in the stirring times of war, but also in the quiet years of profound peace, our sailors are heroes. It was only after years of perfect preparation and absolute readiness for any emergency, that the opportunity came to Dewey in the harbor of Manila, and to Hobson off Santiago de Cuba. It is no diminution of their glory to say that there were others as brave and as ready for high service and noble sacrifice as they. The life of this young Ensign offers no slight evidence of this. Sound must the system of training be which produces such men. And happy the people from whom they spring.

It is a striking coincidence that just at this moment the government, in increasing its naval armament, should give to two of its new vessels the names of two young Kentuckians who, at the very threshhold of young manhood, gave their lives at the call of duty in the navy. Hugh McKee, and John Talbot, were each of them about twenty-six years of age, when they rendered the single service which has made their names thus to live in the annals of our country. Both of them were well fitted to illustrate the unwillingness of men to let any noble deed be forgotten. May these pages do something to perpetuate and keep green the memory of the loyal boy whose life they attempt to portray.

CHAPTER I

BIRTH AND PARENTAGE

'' Blazoned as on heaven's immortal noon
The Cross leads generations on.''

Shelley.

JOSEPH CABELL BRECKIN-RIDGE was born at Fortress Monroe, Virginia, March 6, 1872. But though he was born in Virginia, he was, save for this "accident of birth," a Kentuckian. It was only because his father, Lieutenant Joseph Cabell Breckinridge, an officer in the Second Artillery, happened to be stationed at Fortress Monroe, that he was born in the "Old Dominion." On the other hand, by all the deep-seated tendencies of blood and environment, and by the choice of his mature manhood when he came to exercise the suffrage of an American citizen, he was identified with the daughter State beyond the mountains. His loyalty to his State was tempered only by the higher loyalty so nobly taught by Kentucky's greatest son. But if with Lincoln he loved his country first, he had a strong affection for the fair little city in the beautiful "Blue Grass region," and even more for the strong and fertile soil of the lovely country round about, which, like Attic Colonus, has been so long famous for its breed of horses and of men.

In the little city of Lexington, Ky., on the street known as Broadway, near the centre of the town, are three houses. They are substantial brick houses in the Southern style. One of them has recently replaced a much older one. These three adjoining houses, occupied by kinsfolk on both sides of his family-tree, one of them in succession by two of his grandfathers; these, with three country places in the county, the old Breckinridge home of "Cabell's Dale," the newer, "Braedalbane," and the Warfield place known as "Grasmere," were Cabell Breckinridge's native land. Across the street from the three old houses was the plain brick church in which his grandfather had ministered; not far away was the imposing bank-building in which another grandfather had long been the reigning power; across the street from the bank was the antique court-house, beloved for its discomforts and decay, where generations of his kinsmen had swayed the fortunes of their fellow-men in legal and political debate; hard by was the broad street, known as " Cheapside," once having a market-place in its centre, since replaced by a bronze statue of John C. Breckinridge, the scene of all the gatherings of the country folk, and redolent with memories of fierce personal discussions closely associated with his family name. If he was not born here, nor even lived here very much, yet here he was bred. So many household memories turned hither, so many longings for the scenes and the kindred here, so magical an attraction lay in the rolling hills crowned with wide trees and carpeted with fragrant grass, that he ever felt that here was his home.

No man's life can be understood without some knowledge of his ancestry. In the case of Cabell Breckinridge the story of his life is simply a page from the history of his family. The Breckinridges were sprung from sturdy Scotch stock. On the return of Charles II. they fled from Ayrshire to the highlands of Argyle and thence passed over into Ireland. About 1730 they came to America, and settled in the Cumberland Valley, in Pennsylvania. From Pennsylvania they moved to Virginia, and from Virginia to Kentucky. Generation by generation they mingled their blood with other vigorous pioneer families, chiefly Scotch and Scotch-Irish, but with more than one strong stream of hardy English blood.[1] The early records of Kentucky are full of the doings of three brothers of the family, Alexander Breckinridge and Gen. Robert Breckinridge of Louisville, and John Breckinridge. The latter at the age of thirty-three removed from Char-

[1] See Fiske's *Old Virginia and Her Neighbors*, vol. ii., p. 28, where the Cabell family is chosen with those of Randolph, Cary, and Lee to illustrate the typical Virginia genealogy.

lottesville, Va., and settled at "Cabell's Dale," about seven miles east of Lexington. He had begun his public career by an election to the Virginia House of Delegates before he was twenty years of age, and after considerable public services resigned from the National House of Representatives upon his removal to Kentucky. His brief career,—for he died in 1806, at the age of forty-six, —saw him render conspicuous services to his State and occupy a seat in the United States Senate and in Mr. Jefferson's Cabinet as Attorney-General. His wife, Mary Hopkins Cabell, was a woman of remarkable gifts. Her brilliant sayings pass current now far beyond the circle of her many descendants, and her vigorous intellect lives to-day in un mistakable characteristics in grandchildren and great-grandchildren.

The third son of John Breckinridge was Robert Jefferson Breckinridge.

LAW OFFICE OF ATTORNEY-GENERAL JOHN BRECKINRIDGE AT CABELL'S DALE. BUILT IN 1793.

His name, if it is now fading from general recollection, was a household word a generation ago. His powerful intellect, fervid speech, and superb courage, made his long life one great battle with every form of falsehood and wrong. Beginning his life as a lawyer, he soon entered public life as a Whig, and served several terms in the legislature. When about twenty-eight years old the faith of his fathers laid hold on him with tremendous force of conviction, and he entered the Presbyterian ministry. As a pastor he was devoted and beloved; as a preacher he was brilliant and admired; as a controversialist he was bold and dreaded: yet he became celebrated for the breadth and learning of his theological writings; was never neglectful of his duty as a public-spirited citizen, and occupied with success positions as editor, college president, Superintendent of Public Instruction, and professor of theology. In the great struggle that convulsed the Southern States, he was a fearless champion of emancipation and union. He was the leader of the emancipation party in Kentucky in 1849, one of the bulwarks of loyalty in 1861, and presided over the Republican National Convention in 1864. His brothers, Hon. Joseph Cabell Breckinridge, the father of Vice-President John C. Breckinridge, Rev. John Breckinridge, D.D., and Rev. William L. Breckinridge, D.D., were worthy representatives of the family.

Robert Jefferson Breckinridge married his cousin, Sophonisba Preston, daughter of General Francis Preston, granddaughter of Colonel William Preston, who died from injuries received at the Battle of Guilford Court-House, and great-granddaughter of that father of the faithful, John Preston, one of the noblest progenitors of a line of God-fearing patriots to be found in the records of our race.[1]

The tenth child, and fifth son, of this marriage, was Joseph Cabell Breckinridge. He was born in Baltimore, Maryland, while his father was pastor of the Second Presbyterian Church of that city, January 14, 1842. Educated at Transylvania University (Ky.), Centre College (Ky.), and the University of Virginia, he was reading law when the war broke out. Though only nineteen years of age he quickly volunteered his services for the maintenance of the Union,

[1] General Francis Preston was a member of Congress under the Articles of Confederation. His wife was the only daughter of Gen. Wm. Campbell, the " Hero of King's Mountain" (1780). Other children were : Senator Wm. Campbell Preston, Gen. John S. Preston, M.C., Thos. L. Preston, Eliza, who married Gen. Edward Carrington, Susan, who married Gov. James McDowell, Maria, who married John M. Preston, Sally, who married Gov. John B. Floyd, and Margaret, who married Gov. Wade Hampton,

and August 30, 1861, he was appointed by General William Nelson, on his staff as Assistant Adjutant-General of the forces then assembling at Camp Nelson. Subsequently he was transferred to the staff of General George H. Thomas, with whom he served until he received a commission (dated April 14, 1862) in the regular army for gallantry at the Battle of Mill Spring. He served with distinction throughout the war, was captured at the time and place that General McPherson was killed, before Atlanta, and twice brevetted for gallant and meritorious services.[1]

In 1868 Major Breckinridge married Miss Louise Ludlow Dudley, of Lexington, Ky. The Dudleys were among the earliest pioneers of Kentucky, and have given a number of distinguished names to her history. Among these that of Dr. Benjamin

[1] Now Major-General, and Inspector-General in the United States Army.

Dudley, whose reputation as a surgeon is international, and Dr. Ethelbert Ludlow Dudley, are especially notable. Dr. Ethelbert Dudley was a man of rare and pervading personality. Every one who knew him loved him ; he mingled with every class in society, from the highest to the lowest, with equal ease ; he had a peculiar influence over animals, and the same power of attaching them to him that he had over men. He was a surgeon of the highest skill, a general practitioner of unusual acceptability, a lecturer of high popularity both in the medical department of Transylvania University, at Lexington, and the Louisville University. Besides this he was a man of fine literary taste, a wide reader, and a discriminating critic. He always took an active part in public affairs, was a political leader, and when the Civil War broke out he at once became the organizer of the loyal element for military service in the nation's cause. He raised the 21st Regiment of Kentucky Volunteers, and became its commanding officer. But unhappily his life was cut short February 20, 1862, by camp fever.

Col. Ethelbert L. Dudley married Miss Mary Dewees Scott, daughter of Matthew T. Scott, of Lexington, Ky. Matthew T. Scott emigrated from Shippensburg, in Pennsylvania. and soon impressed himself on the community as a business man of unusual ability and the highest probity. He became the president of the Northern Bank of Kentucky, which with its branches in various towns was by far the most powerful financial institution in all that section of country. The history of this bank is unique in the financial history of the Middle West, where so many " wild-cat " schemes at more than one period flourished, and the period of Matthew T. Scott's presidency is inferior to none for intelligence and soundness of administration.

The only children of Col. Ethelbert L. Dudley were Matthew Scott Dudley, who entered the army with his father, and soon after the war met an accidental death, and Mrs. Breckinridge.

One thing remains to be noted in connection with this ancestry. In every line, in addition to high intellectual gifts, strong personality and lofty patriotism, we find intense religious convictions. All these families are of old Calvinistic creed. The Bible is to all of them the Word of God, the Westminister Standards a sufficient statement of their faith, the Shorter Catechism, especially, a perfect *vade mecum* of early education. None of the children of these households but can recall the Sabbath afternoon drill, often including the Scripture proof texts. If there was any drudgery about it, it was too early in youth to becloud the memory of the hasty repetition of the familiar phrases. An anecodote of General Breckinridge well illustrates this teaching.

Some years ago General Breckinridge was standing on the street in Denver, Colorado, when he noticed that a gentleman in passing looked at him very closely. He turned and followed the gentleman with his eye, who looked back and seeing he had been observed retraced his steps and walking up to General Breckinridge said to him : " What is the chief end of man ? " The instant response was : " Man's chief end is to glorify God and enjoy Him forever." The questioner held out his hand and said : " I knew by your look and carriage that you were an army officer and a Presbyterian."

In such families our age has inherited and preserved something of

the splendor of the time when
freedom was a thing to be fought for,
not to be enjoyed in ease and idleness.
They have continued to realize that
the dearest freedom is freedom to
worship God according to every
man's conscience. And their con-
sciences have bowed before the
authority of God's will. More than
once they have become "strangers
and pilgrims" for the sake of faith
and freedom. They have held
wealth and all worldly prosperity of
little worth in comparison with the
claims of country and of conscience.
Over against the soft allurements of
nineteenth-century philosophy, with
its shibboleth of sweetness and light,
they have repeated the old-time
watchwords of faith and frugality;
they have even dared to defy the
cynical rationalism of the day with
the old war-cry, "Thus saith the
Lord"; and whatever else may have
befallen them they have not failed to

see, generation by generation, fulfilments of the promise, " Know, therefore, that the Lord thy God He is God, the faithful God which keepeth covenant and mercy with them that love Him and keep His commandments to a thousand generations."

To many a man ancestral influences are only silent tendencies. They operate upon him according to the laws of heredity, determining his actions only as they determine his stature.　But it was not so with Cabell Breckinridge.　His family had the Scotch character of clanishness. Though scattered broadly over the continent, though divided by radical differences of taste and temper, though sometimes bitterly antagonizing each other on public questions, they clung together, talked much of each other and the forebears of their name, and in a spirit of love rather than pride of race, kept alive the sayings and doings of the past.　His

ancestry looked down upon his boyhood like a great cloud of witnesses.
He could not but feel that they
demanded of him three things:
First, that he should be a leader;
second, that he should be an outspoken Christian, and, third, that he
should be ready to serve his country
even with his life.

CHAPTER II

BOYHOOD

"The childhood shows the man,
As morning shows the day."
—*Paradise Regained.*

CABELL BRECKINRIDGE
spent the greater portion of
his life prior to his appointment to
the Naval Academy at various military posts. His father was placed in
command of the approaches to
Washington in 1874, with his residence at Fort Foote, eight miles
below Washington. Here he continued to reside until 1878, when he
was ordered to the Washington

Arsenal, where he remained until 1881. From 1881 to 1884 he was stationed at the Presidio, San Francisco, Cal., thus covering the period of his son's childhood. These years were interspersed with visits, often of long duration, to Kentucky. During these years Cabell Breckinridge made the impression upon those who knew him well of a rather delicate boy, of high temper, nervous energy and abundant, if not always well directed, intellectual ability. The influences which surrounded him were those which have been already referred to as hereditary. Not only in his father and mother did he find those intense convictions, which were a part of their inheritance and which had been greatly stimulated by the moral issues which had brought on the war and had carried it to a successful termination, but all about him his relatives and associates were largely of the same temperament.

There was throughout the circle of influences which went to develop his childhood a strong intellectual and moral stimulus. Many of the more intimate friends and relatives with whom he came in contact were men of mark in their several professions and callings, not a few of them of intense ambition, and in some cases of very radical differences of opinion, which led to frequent discussion and debate. He breathed, too, an atmosphere of love of country which was consecrated by the memory of beloved relatives, and given definiteness by his father's profession and his familiarity with his country, resulting from his residence at the capital and his extended travel over it. But most of all he lived in the midst of a true religious devotion and a sincere affection for the church of his fathers and for its traditions. While his education suffered somewhat from the removals from place to place and the want of satisfactory schools in several of the places in which he had lived, the higher education of the boy, the spiritual training which went to make his higher nature, was being richly developed during all these years.

He spent the year 1884-5 during an extended leave of his father's in Lexington, Ky., and from 1885 to 1888 he lived in Chicago. During these years the defects of his early education became manifest, and were only partially rectified by the better educational facilities which this period afforded. It was therefore not without some misgivings that his appointment in 1888 as a naval cadet was received by many of those who were intimately acquainted with him. He had all the qualities that were necessary for the making of a true man. He had already united with the Presbyterian church; his outspoken candor was a conspicuous feature of his character; and his ability was known to be more than equal to the requirements of the course which he was about to enter upon. But on the other hand, the slight figure, the nervous temperment, and the somewhat undisciplined temper of the lad of sixteen seemed hardly fitted for the rigorous routine and severe discipline of the Academy.

Despite this fact, the appointment having been offered to him by his father's elder brother, Colonel Wm. C. P. Breckinridge, then member of Congress, and it not being certain that he would have another opportunity to follow out a career which was already strongly attractive to him, it was decided that he should accept it. About this time his father was appointed Brigadier-General, and became the chief of the Inspector-General's department, with which he had been connected since 1881. This brought his family to Washington, a circumstance which, with his strong family affection, did much to make the life at Annapolis a happy one. After a short time spent at Annapolis under the instruction of a coach, Cabell Breckinridge passed the entrance examinations, and in September, 1888, became a naval cadet.

The impression made on other boys at this time is worthy of a brief notice. One comrade of his life in California, the son of another army officer, writes :

" I regret that my friendship with Cabell began and ended when we were both so young at the Presidio. I have never seen him since, though I used to hear a great deal of him. . . . I can understand how the kindness he used to show toward the littlest boys, and the reckless good spirits and daring which we older little boys admired and tried to emulate, were the essentials which later made him the first among officers and gentlemen. He has left the memory among all who knew him of a most loving and lovable nature."

Another writes:

" I knew Cabell well in his childhood. He was one of those children who are called ' unfortunate ' because so often hurt. As is usually the case there was little of ' fortune ' or mere ' chance ' in it. His was a nervous, eager, impatient temper, and he was quite reckless of consequences. He always bore the ' consequences ' like a soldier. I remember his having received a very bad cut over the eye in some rough play when a boy of eight, and how well he bore the pain during the long time that elapsed before the surgeon came. About the same time he showed remarkable coolness when his father was injured by the explosion of a cartridge, carrying the news to his mother with a *sang-froid* which prevented undue alarm, and watching the surgeon in his treatment of the wound, which was a serious one in the shoulder, with the utmost composure."

And another says :

" My first meeting with Cabell Breckinridge was rather a bashful affair on both sides, as I remember it through the lapse of sixteen years. As sons of officers in the Regular Army of the United States, stationed at the Presidio, the garrison near San Francisco, Cal., we formed a boyhood friendship such as only the unrestricted freedom of the children's life at an army post can form. And though in the last twelve years I have seen Breckinridge but seldom, the knowledge of his progress in life, of his actions and ambitions, has been often brought before me through the medium of relatives, his classmates at Annapolis, and his fellow-officers in the service, so that when the news of his death at the post of duty off the shore of Cuba was sent to the government at Washington, the friendship of the past recurred distinctly, and seemed to reach in an unbroken line down to the present time.

"As I knew him, Cabell Breckinridge, with his high-strung nature—strong in its attachments and its aversions, quick to aid where help was needed, and as quick to resent injury or fancied wrong,— showed plainly the fighting stock of which he came. Reckless and daring as a lad, he was in no sense quarrelsome, and his differences were generally in behalf of his friends, and not with them. He was always ready for sport of any kind, and while never very athletic, he made up in grit and courage what he lacked in simple physical strength. Oftentimes sport took the form of mischief, of more or less serious degree; but it can never be said that any vicious motive influenced the boyish actions which must form a part of the nature of any lad of spirit and good birth. He believed in fair play at all times, and held that the violation of a promise was an inexcusable fault.

"He was not a good student, but nevertheless learned quickly, and put the knowledge acquired aptly to use when occasion presented. Of the last twelve years of his life I have, as I have said before, known but little personally; yet, from his classmates, and his brother-officers in the service, I know that he was accounted a man of courage and of loyalty to his friends, and I think no one will contradict me in saying that by his death the Navy has lost a gallant officer— one who would not have been found wanting in the hour of need, nor in the discharge of his duty."

CHAPTER III

AT THE NAVAL ACADEMY

" Just at the age 'twixt boy and youth
When thought is speech, and speech is truth."
—*Marmion.*

THE materials for this part of
Cabell Breckinridge's life con-
sist chiefly in the recollections of
some of his contemporaries. The
following graphic letter by a classmate of the class of 1892, leaves little to be desired as a pen-portrait :

" I first met Cabell in August,
1888, at Mr. R. L. Werntz's preparatory school in Annapolis, where we
were both studying for the Naval

Academy entrance examinations. We soon knew each other, and from the first, I think, decided to be friends ; and such we continued throughout the four years at the Academy, and after that until the end. We entered in September, and that part of the class was quartered on board the old *Santee*, the ' May plebes' being still away—no, I am wrong; they had just returned from their summer cruise, and we all lived together during September, the three upper classes being on leave.

"With the first of October the academic year began, and from that time on I saw a great deal of Cabell ; we were not roommates, but lived near together on the first floor of the New Quarters. I was often with him in the section room, at drills (we were in the same company), and during leisure hours, so I soon got to know him well, and to like him more and

more.   He was full of mischief
and high spirits, always skylarking
and playing practical jokes, and never
so happy as when engaged in a rough-
and-tumble wrestling match with a
crowd of classmates in somebody's
room or around the corridors.   He
was tall and slender for his age, but
not weak or sickly; on the contrary
he seemed as tough as wire, and his
activity and energy were tireless.   I
have said that Cabell was a great
practical joker, but he never de-
scended to a mean trick; he was
frank and open about what he did,
always, and took a joke as well as he
played it.   He was rather hot-headed
by nature, but even when angry his
generosity never failed him, and he
soon forgot the cause of the outburst.
I remember that once, when we were
plebes, Cabell and Mr. Crank had a
dispute about something at the
table (I forget what), and in true
boyish fashion they agreed that they

must fight it out.   Mr. Rodney, who
roomed with Cabell, and I did our
best to laugh the matter down, and
failing in that, to reason the two out
of their determination.   But no ;
both were proud and fancied themselves 'insulted,' and nothing could
stop them.   So Rodney was Cabell's
second and I was Crank's, and we
went behind the armory, where the
affair was soon settled.   None of
the four knew anything about such
matters I think, and I know that no
harm was done on either side.   After
it was over all animosity instantly
vanished ; the fighters shook hands,
and from that day were better
friends than ever, and never to my
knowledge had another falling out.
Rodney and I were rejoiced at such
a conclusion, for our sympathies had
been about equally divided all along.

   "When we became 'youngsters,'
or third-class men, Cabell was soon
known by all the new plebes as one

of the most merciless 'runners' in the Academy; but not one of them ever bore him the slightest ill-will on that account, I am sure. The kind of hazing that we did was mild and harmless—in fact, I am convinced that we were all benefited by what we received, and so were those who came after us. Cabell was very ingenious in devising new schemes of running to try on the fourth-class men, and we all—plebes included—got a great deal of fun out of them. Here again, however, there was nothing of the bully or coward in what he did; for although he himself had suffered a good deal from the persecution of certain upper-class bullies while he was a plebe, he was too high-minded to resort to such tactics when the opportunity was given him.

"He was always fearless and independent, whether among his equals or those above him—cadets or offi-

cers—and very tenacious of what he
believed to be his rights; he resented
any act of injustice and imposition,
and never suffered it tamely or cring-
ingly. But there was nothing sul-
len about his disposition; if he was
harshly or unfairly treated, he made
known his feelings promptly, and had
it out, so to speak, then and there.
I think it was this trait that made
him liked by everyone except bullies, who feared him for it.

"He often got into scrapes of one
sort or another, chiefly through his
reckless and fun-loving nature, which
prompted him to commit innumerable petty breaches of the regulations
(most of which were made only to
be broken, anyhow). If he was discovered, he got demerits for these
mild offences, of course, and the
sum of them for a month was usually
enough to put him in a low 'conduct grade,' although he had done
nothing, in reality, to deserve it.

This necessarily told heavily against him in class standing, for what they call 'conduct and discipline' at the Naval Academy is given more weight than almost anything else. Cabell would laugh over his troubles, and every now and then honestly resolve to keep off the conduct report in future. Sometimes he would be successful for a week or so, but never much longer; his restless spirit would lead him, often with the utmost innocence, into some new escapade, which, harmless as it always was, and generally comical, would end in his name appearing again on the report.

"During the two years or more that we were in the same class this unlucky propensity was strongest; for he was then very young—one of the youngest men in the class—and had n't begun to take things seriously. He was always ready to drop everything for a friendly tussle or race in the corridor, and often his recitations suffered in consequence. He had so many friends, and spent so large a part of his time with them, that there was not much left for study. This was the sole cause of his failure to keep up with the class, as was shown by his record in the class of '95, when he had grown more serious and thoughtful; for as soon as he began really to apply himself, he showed at once what was in him, and took high rank in most of his studies.

" Cabell was always an enthusiast on the subject of athletics, and not in theory only, or chiefly; he became especially interested in boxing while we were plebes, and practised in the gymnasium as often as he could get the opportunity, soon developing into one of the best boxers in the class. He was not, of course, power-fully built; but his body and limbs were tough and elastic, his head and nerves steady and under perfect control, and he was as quick as a flash to seize an advantage when it was offered. These are the very qualities that make a born fencer, and such he proved himself to be when, a little later, we were given our first lessons by Mr. Corbesier, the swordmaster. Cabell showed a preference, at the start, for the foils over the broadswords, and from that time on was most constant and diligent in his sword-practice. He quickly passed all the rest of us, and became the brave old master's favorite pupil. During part of the year cadets were allowed and encouraged to take extra lessons in the armory, between supper and the call to evening studies; and Cabell, especially during the latter part of his course, was to be seen nearly every evening of the week devoting that hour to his favorite pursuit, working away with untiring zeal and energy to perfect himself in this branch of his profes-

sion. Mr. Corbesier took a deep
interest in such a promising and
faithful scholar, and helped him on
by every means in his power; he
loved him for himself, too, and
treated him with a sort of fatherly
kindness and affection that was
almost pathetic.

"When I left the Academy, in
1892, Cabell had become a skilful
fencer; but at the time of his graduation, in 1895, he was recognized as
by far the most expert swordsman
of the battalion of cadets, and his
instructors declared that few, if any,
who were his equals had ever been
graduated. He took a prominent
part in the exhibition tournaments
held from time to time, and his
fencing was always regarded as *the*
part of the entertainment not to be
missed.

"In connection with this subject
I will mention an incident that perhaps you know of already, though

Cabell's modesty was such that he
may well have failed to talk about
it, even to you; this happened after
I left, and has been told me by Mr.
Cushman, an ensign on board this
ship.

"Cabell and three of his classmates—Mr. Walker (J. E.), Mr.
Cushman, and Mr. Johnson—had
just finished an exhibition of fencing
at a tournament in the old gymnasium. As they were going down-
stairs, after dressing, Mr. Corbesier
called the party, and holding out
his cap to them, told each one to
draw a slip of paper from it. Without a word each took a slip,
and on examining them, Cabell's
was found to have a mark on it.
The old gentleman then stepped
aside, and presently appeared with a
pair of beautiful gold-chased duel-
ling swords, which he presented to
Cabell, saying that he had been un-
willing to make a choice among the

four (the best pupils he had), and
had thus left the decision to chance.
It was well known that he would
have singled out Cabell without a
moment's hesitation as the one most
worthy of the gift, but for his unwillingness to hurt the others' feelings ; and he was plainly delighted
at the result, which was just what
he so earnestly wished.

"The three other fellows shook
hands with Cabell and congratulated
him in all sincerity; for they believed, and have said ever since, that
the swords went to the man that,
beyond question, deserved them.

"This same team continued to
lead the Academy in the art of fencing, but Cabell was easily pre-emi-
nent among them to the last.   ·

"He was an ardent lover of foot-
ball, too, and in spite of his light
weight, was a very good player ;
during his first-class year he was, I
believe, on the Academy eleven for a

time, and was always considered a
first-rate ' end,' on account of his
quickness, speed, and endurance.
He was hurt several times in playing; not seriously, but enough to
lay him off for a while; and towards
the end of the season I think, he
gave up the game almost entirely,
being anxious to prevent any accident that might interfere with his
studies and keep him from finishing
his course with credit.

" Of Cabell's social life at Annapolis I cannot say much, as it did
not begin, properly speaking, until
he was a second-class man, when I
had gone away; I mean, of course,
the round of society life as it exists
at the Naval Academy, and of which
third- and fourth-class men saw little
when I was there. But Cabell had
always a few friends, both among
the officers' families and out in the
town, whom he used to visit, even
the first year. One house that was

constantly open to him, and which
he loved to visit, was the C———s' ;
and I remember going there with
him, when we were plebes, and meeting Mrs. C———, who is a relative
of yours, is she not? Cabell was
extremely fond of her, and frequently
spent a Saturday evening or a Sun-
day afternoon at the house. I went
several times, and from the first was
much impressed by her gentleness
and kind hospitality, as well as by
her beauty, of which Cabell was
justly very proud, she being his
cousin and a Kentuckian.

"Out in Annapolis the K———s
were his especial friends, in those
days, and I think they continued to
be throughout his whole course.
When he had liberty on Saturday
afternoons he usually spent part of
his time, at least, at their house;
Mrs. K——— was especially fond
of him, and in her motherly way
contributed a great deal to his com-

fort and happiness, I know. There, too, he often met his friends from Washington, Baltimore, and elsewhere when they came to visit Annapolis; and you know better than I how glad he always was when any of his family or their friends came over to see him. He was like a caged animal when they were out in town, and he was not allowed to leave the yard; and I have known him on several occasions to "french" out anyhow to see them, even when a very few demerits more would make his case a serious one. I need not tell you that this was one of his most prominent traits, loyalty to home and friends. He must have had his family constantly in his thoughts, for he talked to me a great deal of them.

"But it was his nature to be loyal, and this nature was often shown to those outside of the home circle; his friendship was of the genuine sort, not easily shaken, constant through thick and thin. He never betrayed a friend, come what might; and I have known him to get into trouble time and again through his efforts to help some other fellow out of a scrape. His generosity was perfect; all that he had he was willing, and more than willing, to share with his friends—not ostentatiously, but simply and naturally, as if no other thought could enter his mind. And the honest faithfulness of his friendship was shown by the trust he placed in those who trusted him as a friend."

The peculiarities of disposition, which we need not hesitate to call faults, noted in the foregoing letter, brought Cabell Breckinridge more than once under discipline and threatened at one time to break off his course at the Academy once for all. But through the generous aid of influential friends he was rein-

stated, and eventually graduated in
the class of 1895. He was one of
those boys whom every teacher
knows well ; boys to be worked over,
grieved over, yet confidently believed
in ; boys who are sound in essentials, but lawless in the lesser matters of discipline which detract from
a boy's character neither as a gentleman nor a Christian, but often pro-
duce endless discord and unrest. It
takes time to teach such boys that
he who is to command well must
know how to obey implicitly. It
takes time, but they learn it in the
end. How well Cabell Breckenridge
learned it the following incident will
show.

In a recent letter Lieutenant-
Commander Kimball, of the *Dupont*,
in speaking of him, says:

" He used to dine and lunch aboard
this boat frequently, and as you may
imagine was always a most welcome

guest.   A characteristic action of Breckinridge's was this.   A late change in uniform requires shoulder-straps to be worn on the overcoat. The rest of us made the severe wear on clothes an excuse for disregarding the order more or less, on the ground that since we were not required to have frock coats that take straps, we need not have these on the over-coats.   Breckinridge wore his and when we chaffed him said with that attractive, quiet smile of his : ' Well, its regulation and its not my lookout if its stupid.' "

The development of the dash and daring which were always a part of his character is seen in the readiness with which he faced danger in these years.   During his vacation in the summer of 1893 he joined his family at Fisher's Island, in Long Island Sound.   While there two men went in swimming just as a storm was coming up, and soon became exhausted by the force of the waves. They got on the diving raft, but it was soon torn from its anchorage, and was being borne out to sea, when Cabell Breckinridge called his younger brother, Ethelbert, and taking a boat they went to the aid of the men, and succeeded in bringing them safely to the shore.

During the storm above-mentioned the island was cut off from communication with the shore, and a child suffering from diphtheria was deprived of medical services. The Breckinridge boys volunteered to nurse the child, and when the physician, who had been caught on shore, returned, he said that only the presence of mind, prompt action, and careful nursing which they had given had saved the child's life.

He saved another person from drowning at Annapolis shortly before his graduation in 1895. A gentleman fell overboard in the harbor, and with characteristic quickness of thought and action he sprang to the rescue.

But he had something more than physical courage. He had all the high loyalty to truth which marks the Christian gentleman. . He was not ashamed of his faith, though as far as possible from a hypocrite. ‑Frank and outspoken in this as in all else, he was just as much and as naturally a Christian and a Presbyterian as he was an American and a Kentuckian. The words of Doddridge's beautiful hymn in the old Psalm-book had risen too often for him and his not to find an answer. And when he was formed, its prayer

"" God of our fathers, be the God
Of their succeeding race,"

was, so far as he was concerned, fulfilled. A classmate says :

" He rarely spoke of matters religious, yet from his lips came the most beautiful defence, or rather explanation, of the Presbyterian belief that ever put scoffing cadet to retraction of his flippancy."

On one occasion, when under inquiry for complicity in " hazing," he refused to make any concealment of his conduct that would involve any untruth, and Captain Sigsbee bears tribute to his manly conduct during the course of the investigation. He says:

" My acquaintance with [him], save by reputation, was limited to one single noble act and example on his part when we were at the Naval Academy together; an act that I have often called attention to in the service since. I was president of a hazing court in which the tendency to withhold evidence on the part of some of the cadets was most dangerously near the point of dishonor. Finally, in [his] case, a witness testified that he (a very religious boy) had been visited by [young Breckinridge] and told to say the whole truth to the court without respect to its effect on [his] future. It was a most gratifying act to the court, and I never lost a chance to mention it in the Academic Board in [his] favor. Lieutenant Gleaves informs me that the act in view was indicative of [his] whole service career."

Six feet two inches tall, an accomplished swordsman and horseman, with all the attraction of person which comes from good birth and breeding, he left the old Academy where he had spent so many and withal such happy years, with joyous anticipations of the freer life of the sailor afloat, and the larger usefulness of the officer in the actual exercise of his profession.

CHAPTER IV

IN ACTIVE SERVICE

" Great thoughts, great feelings, came to them,
Like instincts, unawares."
—*Milnes.*

CABELL BRECKINRIDGE
completed his course at the
Naval Academy in June, 1895. Under the present regulations he remained a naval cadet for two more
years, spent on board ship. He had
already been for the usual period on
board the practice ships, those to
which he was assigned being the
Constellation and the *Monongahela.*
He was ordered to the receiving-

THE BATTLESHIP "TEXAS."

(FROM A COPYRIGHT PHOTOGRAPH BY WM. H. RAU.)

ship *Vermont*, June 24, 1895, and
remained on board till July 24, 1895,
when he was assigned to the *Mont-
gomery*. He was transferred on
October 12th of the same year to
the *Texas*. His assignment to the
Texas bears date of October 14,
1895. The *Texas*, however, met
with an accident in January, 1896,
which required her to be docked,
and from February 1 to July 20,
1896, Cabell Breckinridge was on
board the ill-fated *Maine*.

During these months of practical
experience of the true demands of
the arduous profession which he had
chosen he was shifted from ship to
ship to a somewhat unusual degree.
He had the opportunity thereby of
meeting an unusual number of officers, and he seems to have won in a
very remarkable degree the confidence and esteem of all who met
him. The service, moreover, which
he saw was more than ordinarily

trying. He used laughingly to de-
clare that the government had done
all in its power to dispose of him.
He had been sent to Bar Harbor to
spend the winter, and to Florida for
the summer. What climatic expos-
ure could not do, he said, was threatened by the vessels themselves.
Referring especially to the torpedo-
boat *Cushing*, on which he served
after his promotion, he said such
craft ought to be dangerous to an
enemy, they were so dangerous to
those on board them. He had several hard experiences in the winter
of 1896–7, which was marked by such
severe gales on the coast. But these
difficulties only developed his character and showed the resources of
his now rapidly expanding manhood.

Of this period of his life one of
his fellow-officers says :

"Cabell made a reputation for
himself that was most enviable. He

was an efficient, practical officer, and was very highly regarded by all the officers, I think without exception, under whom he served. This is the more remarkable because, on one ship at least, a cadet's life was a pretty disagreeable one, the executive officer being a particularly hard man to please, or even to get along with. Cabell worked hard and faithfully there, however, and by his zeal and ability won the highest praise from this same officer, as well as from his commanding officer."

Not only was the respect and friendship of his brother-officers quickly won and firmly held, but he had that surest test of efficiency, that highest proof of capacity for leadership, the power of winning the confidence and affection of the men under his command. On more than one occasion he was ordered to take a volunteer crew on some dangerous and difficult duty.   So ready was the response to every call he made that it was never a question who would go with, but only whom he would take with him.

The details of some of his gallant acts are unfortunately not easily obtained.   A casual mention in a letter home, a general impression in the memory of a comrade, a bluff but tender word from some admiring seaman, like the old Greek, Venis, who rejoiced to follow him, are the only data that are available.   From these fragmentary records we glean the following incidents:

During the severe storm which swept the Atlantic coast in February, 1896, Cabell Breckinridge, then on board the *Maine*, was off Old Point Comfort.   Much damage was done all along the coast by this storm, and the " White Squadron " was in especial peril, and more than one gallant act was reported.   About ten o'clock one night the executive officer was notified that a launch had gone adrift. He at once summoned Cadet Breckinridge, who was not on duty, and directed him to obtain a volunteer crew, man a boat, and recover the launch. It was a very stormy night, the wind was blowing a gale, and sheets of rain and sleet filled the air. He had no trouble in selecting from those who volunteered a thoroughly capable crew, and they set out on their perilous quest. It was not without difficulty that the lost launch was discovered in the darkness, and it was only by the most exhausting labors that at last, in the gray dawn of the winter morning, the worn-out crew were gotten on board and their task successfully achieved. On this, as on some other occasions, Venis was his right-hand man.

About this time, during a storm, an urgent call was signalled from Fort-

ress Monroe for a priest. The Roman Catholic priest of the post was
absent, and a sick man was urgent
for spiritual ministration. The storm
was so severe that there was great
hesitancy about sending ashore
Father Chidwick, the chaplain of the
Maine. But with that devotion to
duty which he so beautifully exhibited at Havana when the *Maine* was
destroyed, Father Chidwick was
ready to take any risk. With the
broad religious sympathy which in
his family has always been coupled
with intense devotion to his own
faith, Cabell Breckinridge volunteered his services, and the old Greek
headed the crew, and Scotch Presbyterian and Greek Catholic took the
Roman priest on his stormy voyage
of religious consolation.

Perhaps the promptitude and energy of his character was never better shown than by an incident which
occurred on the *Texas.* Ammuni-

tion was being hoisted from the magazine to the gun-deck. Just as it reached the deck where it was to be used the hoist failed to work, and instead of the load being swung around and delivered on the deck, it began to fall rapidly. Had the ammunition fallen into the magazine from such a height at such speed, an explosion would have been inevitable, and the stately ship would have gone down with none to tell how she met her end. But the young cadet, seeing the failure of the hoist to perform its proper function, seeing the ammunition start on its swift descent, flung himself upon the load as it passed him and dashed it aside, landing it safely on the deck. He was caught, however, in the shoulder by the machinery and thrown to one side. One of the men cried, " My God, Mr. Breckinridge has had his arm torn off ! " By rare good fortune this proved not to be the case.　His clothing gave way and only the sleeve of his coat was torn away.[1]

[1] Mr. Winston Churchill, in an article upon the destruction of Cervera's fleet in the " Battle of the 3d of July," published in the August number of *The Review of Reviews*, makes this striking reference to Cabell Breckinridge, referring particularly to the above-mentioned episode :

" The brightest side of the simple character of our American sailor—the side upon which the people love best to dwell—is his tenderness, his bigness of heart.　His strong arm is ever ready to sustain the helpless.　Even in times of peace rarely a week passes aboard the ships that death is not braved to save a comrade.　Some of this reaches the press, but the most of it does not. Could the short life be written of Ensign Breckinridge, who was swept off the *Cushing* as she was going to Havana before the war and died after his rescue, many a gilt-edged biography would pale in comparison.　But three years out of the Academy, he had taken six drowning men from the sea.　Once, when he was standing on the deck of the *Texas*, the ammunition hoist gave way and the shot began falling into the powder.　From the edge of the hatch Mr. Breckinridge threw himself at the running bunch of strands and was carried around and around until his clothes were torn from his body and his

Two years fly very swiftly amid such changing scenes, and their end found the young naval cadet thoroughly in love with his profession. There had been times in his life at Annapolis when he was inclined to question the wisdom of his choice, and to look with something of longing in his glance upon other professions. But he had grown rapidly in the two years on shipboard, and had come to full manhood. He now realized the meaning of the many demands the preliminary training of the naval officer makes upon youth, and was resolved to show his ability to satisfy those demands to the full. In such a spirit he left the *Texas* late in April, 1897, and returned to Annapolis.

hands and arms were stripped and bleeding. But there was no explosion. And he was one of many. The charity that belittles all else is the creed of ward-room and steerage and forecastle, where the man without money is he who has the most."

CHAPTER V

ON BOARD THE "CUSHING"

> " To this military attitude of the soul we give the name of Heroism. Its rudest form is the contempt for safety and ease which makes the attractiveness of war. It is a self trust which slights the restraints of prudence, in the pleni-tude of its energy and power to repair the harms it may suffer."
>
> *—Emerson.*

CABELL BRECKINRIDGE returned to Annapolis for his final examinations for promotion to the rank of Ensign early in May, 1897. His two years of service afloat had done much to develop his character and give breadth and consistency to

THE TORPEDO-BOAT "CUSHING."

his plans for the future. He had lost much of the spirit of reckless indifference to regulations and had come to realize the importance of definite effort as well as general excellence in the career which he had chosen. He therefore set about his examinations with much more interest and application than he had ever shown before. He expressed his confidence in his ability to do much better than he had ever done under similar circumstances, and the consciousness that he had gained the respect and good-will of all with whom he had served did much to stimulate him to earnest effort. The result was all that could have been desired. He was highly complimented by his examiners upon his proficiency, he improved his standing many points, and took a much higher place in the roll of officers of the same standing with himself. It was a real vindication, if any were needed, of the ability which he possessed and which had been obscured during his academy days by his indifference to his record of conduct and discipline.

As soon as his examinations were over and the question of assignment became a definite one, he found several positions open to him; but especial friendship having sprung up with Lieutenant Albert Gleaves, the commander of the torpedo-boat *Cushing*, Lieutenant Gleaves asked that he be assigned to his boat. Breckinridge readily consented to this appointment, which was made. It was an assignment that would not have been sought by many a young officer, as the torpedo service is far less attractive than service on board one of the larger ships. There is not only less companionship and more work, but there are a great number of discomforts incident to the cramped quarters on board the boats, and the real suffering occa-

sioned by any long passage, especially if in a rough sea. Thus, for
instance, on one occasion when going up the coast the *Cushing* met
with such heavy weather that for
sixteen hours the crew were without
food or sleep and the discomforts
caused by the cramped quarters
were very great. In addition to all
this, there was the danger of accident
because of the low bulwark on such
a boat and the frequency with which
it is swept by the sea, and also the
perilous service which it is required
to render in time of war. He, however, took little heed of such matters.
It was in the line of duty, the invita-
tion was an honorable one, and the
association pleasant ; and from July
15, 1897, until February 11, 1898, he
served on board the *Cushing*, winning
the affection and esteem of his commanding officer .and the devotion of
her crew. How well he conducted
himself may be gathered from some

of the tributes of those best qualified to judge. Thus, for instance, Lieutenant-Commander W. W. Kimball, commanding the torpedo-boat flotilla, says:

" He was always ready for any duty ; eager for that which carried danger with it, and quickly responsive to the call of that which could only be tedious and disagreeable. I have seen him jump into the engine room when apparently there was imminent danger of death by scalding, find and rectify the difficulty, restore confidence to the men below, and return on deck with a quiet smile, perfectly unconscious of the fact that anything remarkable had been done. I have known of other instances of the kind.

" When in occasional command of the *Cushing*, the fine seaman-like way in which he handled her demanded and received our sincerest admiration. The resourcefulness with which he met and overcame the many difficulties arising in torpedo-boat service excited our wonder and delight.

" His high sense of duty, his nobility of character as a man and as an officer, drew us to him very closely."

Commander Kimball has also preserved a letter addressed to him by a Presbyterian minister of Miami, Florida, which throws a side-light upon the life which he led during this service, depicting it from a wholly outside point of view. Rev. W. W. Faris writes as follows :

" MY DEAR MR. KIMBALL :

" I am greatly grieved to hear of Mr. Breckinridge's death. By the published accounts it appears that death seized him fronting, with simple, manly courage, the perils of ordinary duty under uncommon emergency. Such a death is as heroic as though encountered in battle : faithful service is not contingent on circumstance for its nobility. It is the man who can be counted on every day, in humdrum routine, who rises to occasion when occasion calls, however unexpected the form in which the call comes.

" I had little thought when at the banquet I alluded to the superiority of living *well* over living *long*, and to the fact that the Navy teaches us all the lesson that we are under orders from a Superior, that illustration such as this would come so soon and so strikingly.

" I had the pleasure of meeting Mr. Breckinridge on deck that morning, and of a few moments' pleasant converse with him. He seemed to me a straightforward, manly, earnest man, without either false or careless ring in his speech—a worthy scion of the distinguished family to which he belonged, and as worthy a member of the honorable profession in whose service he laid down his life."

In the course of the winter more than one trying service fell to the young Ensign's lot. On one occasion the *Cushing* shipped a heavy sea, which swept him off his feet; but he was fortunate enough to catch the life-lines, which in this case proved strong and did not give way, as on a later occasion they were destined to do. Throughout all these months of hard service he devoted himself with uncomplaining vigor to every task until his superior officers had to admonish him that he was overtaxing his strength by excessive zeal. Such, unfortunately, was the case, and it is more than likely that when, on the morning of February 11th, the *Cushing* set sail from Key West for Havana, he was below a normal condition of strength.

Thus Lieutenant - Commander
Kimball, in a letter bearing date
March 26, 1898, says:

" Before we parted company with
the *Cushing* we none of us liked
Breck's looks, and several of us
cautioned him about overworking.
Indeed, Gleaves rebuked him for
working himself down, and insisted
upon his having medical advice.
Breckinridge said he was a bit stale,
or words to that effect, and scoffed
at the idea of his working too hard ;
but took medical advice, and used a
tonic. For myself, I did not like the
way he acted at St. Augustine, in
that he did not go in for the social
amusement as I would have liked to
see him do. However, he was always
rather quiet and dignified, and his
action there made no deep impression.

" After arriving here at Key West,
on 31st December, the *Cushing* had

seven days' work on repairs, and Breckinridge was closely attentive to them. He looked haggard and worn to me, but he insisted that he was all right, and that any way he was not working too hard. After I left for Tampa, meeting the *Cushing* return-ing, the *Cushing* had hard duty on despatch work up to the time she left for Havana. Gleaves tells me that Breckinridge looked no more tired, but I imagine that in his un-satisfactory state of strength the duty pulled him more than he knew."

The tragedy which was destined to bring to an untimely end the prom-ising career of this gallant boy can-not better be told than it is told in the letter which the commander of the *Cushing*, Lieutenant Gleaves, penned on the evening of the disas-ter. He writes:

" 9 P.M.
" Torpedo-Boat *Cushing*,
" HAVANA, CUBA,
" February 11, 1898.

" MY DEAR GENERAL BRECKIN-
RIDGE:

" It is with profound grief that I have to inform you of the details concerning the loss of your incomparable son.

" The *Cushing* received orders last night from Admiral Sicard, acting under telegraphic orders from the Navy Department, to proceed to Havana this morning. We left the dock at Key West at 7.10 A.M., running at a speed of fifteen knots. In the straits we found a fresh breeze from E. N. E. and a moderate sea, both wind and sea going down after two heavy rain-squalls. About 11.30 A.M. the breeze freshened again, and the sea became very heavy. About a half-hour after noon the coast of Cuba was sighted, but the sea by that time was so heavy that the

Cushing was brought head to it, or nearly so, and the engine slowed to about nine and a half knots. Your son was standing on the lee side (starboard) forward, just abaft the funnel. I was aft on the same side, by the signal mast. During this time we frequently talked together, I going to him, or he coming aft; twice, when both of us were together near the signal mast, green seas swept over the boat, drenching us both. Extra life-lines had been stretched fore and aft. About 1.30 your son started aft again to speak to me, when suddenly the boat was thrown violently to leeward, and your son was thrown against the life-lines along the rail. He clutched the ridge-rope, which was just above his head, but the copper rope (three eighths inch), which was about on a level with his knees, parted under the strain, and his feet slipping on the wet deck, went from under him;

at the same time he lost hold of the ridge-rope, and went overboard. Just as the accident happened he turned toward me, gave the sweetest smile I ever saw on the face of a man, and disappeared over the side without a sound. The engines were stopped at once and the lee boat cleared away, the ship turning toward your son. At this instant the after boat-davit bent under the weight of the two men who had responded instantly to the cry; the after-fall slacking in consequence of the davit bending lowered the stern of the boat, which another sea immediately half filled, precipitating both of the crew into the water. Orders were given to cut the forward fall to let the boat go clear; one man was hauled on board, the boat turned keel up with the other, who climbed on the keel and attempted to paddle with his hands toward your son, who was now right ahead,

or nearly so, of the boat, the ship
having been turned by the engines
for this purpose. It was now observed that the boat was badly stove,
and the man on it was hauled on
board. The *Cushing* was now close
to your son, who was on his back,
floating and still swimming. A
third life preserver was thrown him,
which fell about three yards from
him ; also a line which fell short. I
sang out to him not to give up, that
we would pick him up, and the *Cushing* was laid close alongside of him.
Just before reaching him, however,
a tremendous breaking sea broke
over him, and when it passed he was
lying on his face with his face under
water. He was not more than thirty
feet distant, and at this moment
John Everetts, gunner's mate, who
had been in the swamped boat, dived
from the forecastle with a line,
reached him, and secured the line
around his body; then Daniel At-

kins, the ship's cook, jumped overboard, and assisted Everetts in
securing the line. Your son and the
two men were now right alongside
of the *Cushing*, and were hauled on
board with great difficulty. I forgot
to say that the instant the cry of
man overboard was given, two life-
preservers were thrown very close to
your son, but his movements were
impeded by his rain clothes. He
got rid of his boots as soon as he
fell, but of course could not divest
himself of his coat; it was the air
under it, however, that kept him
afloat. From the time that the accident happened until the line was
secured around him it was not more
than ten minutes. But it was at
least five minutes more before we
could get him out of the water.
Everything that was possible to do
to resuscitate him was done; everything in the aid to the apparently
drowned was done continuously, but

I am forced to say that I am of the opinion that your son was suffocated before we reached him. It had been expected to reach Havana about 1.30 this P.M., but slowing in the heavy sea, and afterwards the same thing, in order to keep the boat as quiet as possible in the first hour's attempts at resuscitation, caused a great deal of time to be lost, so that we did not reach Havana until 3 P.M., although the fires under the second boiler had been started, and the greatest speed that the sea would permit was used.

"Upon entering the harbor an urgent signal was made to the U. S. S. *Maine* to send her surgeon; her assistant promptly responded, the surgeon being on shore, but Captain Sigsbee, of the *Maine*, sent out messengers for him, and also for an American doctor well known here, Dr. Burgess. The *Maine's* surgeon could not be found for some time, but Dr. Burgess, an elderly man and a practitioner of considerable reputation, was soon on board, and the work of resuscitation which began at 1.45 and had been *uninterruptedly* continued until the arrival of Dr. Burgess, was not abandoned until 5 P.M. Electricity was used, and nothing was left undone."

We can read between the lines of this letter enough to tell how much this young officer had endeared himself to all those with whom he served. His commanding officer has said of him elsewhere, that he was one of the most zealous and efficient officers in the navy, and that he was loved alike by men and officers; that in all his experience he had never seen such devotion as was shown by the crew of the *Cushing* at the time of the accident. Speaking for himself he says: "I loved him for his fearless candor, for his noble quali-

ties, and his unwavering steadfast-
ness." The conduct of the crew,
exceptional as it was, is more elo-
quent even than these tender words.
It has been wondered at that the
colored cook of the boat should have
ventured his life in such a sea for the
young officer. But Ensign Breckinridge had done him one of those
services which he was so swift and
apt to render, and had saved his life
on one occasion when hunting on
shore, and he had won the fearless
devotion of his humble associate.
In this, as in every instance in his
brief career, he exhibited remarkable
power in winning the affection and
securing the following of all those
whom he was called upon to lead.

A further communication dictated
by the Greek sailor, Venis (with in-
terpolations by the shipmate who
wrote it), who has already been several times referred to, further illustrates this quality.

"U. S. S. *Texas*.

" Off Dry Tortugas, Florida.

"March 10, 1898.

" Sir :

" I have the honor to acknowledge, with much gratitude, the receipt of the copy of the Lexington, Ky., paper containing the account of the funeral services and life incidents of your late esteemed son, Ensign J. C. Breckinridge, U. S. N. Being a seaman and no penman, you will pardon my briefly expressing my sympathy through one of my shipmates.

" As related, I have twice had the honor of assisting your son in saving the life of others and, in my own homely expression, had we been together during his last peril, ' I get him or we both go down together.'

" I know of no greater appreciation of his courage and chivalry than this honest expression of the ' old Greek.'

" Pray believe me, with great sympathy for you in our common loss.

" The Old Greek,
" GEORGE VENIS.

" P. S.   The signature is that of George Venis.

" General J. C. Breckinridge,
" 1314 Connecticut Avenue,
" Washington, D. C."

Every effort at resuscitation having proved vain, the body of the young ensign was borne to the beautiful battleship in the harbor of Havana.   Here a brief burial service was held, Father Chidwick, who had served with him on the ship, making a very beautiful and touching address.

Lieutenant Gleaves writing from the *Cushing* at Key West, Florida, May 7, 1898, pays the following tribute to his young comrade :

"My acquaintance with Midshipman Breckinridge began in the fall of 1895, when he was ordered to the U. S. S. *Texas*. He was assigned to my division of great guns, as one of the junior officers, and served as such for fifteen months. During this period of routine service he won the confidence and admiration of all his seniors by the faithfulness and zeal with which he performed his duties, often under most trying circumstances. A Midshipman's life at best on a large ship is full of trials, his duties are innumerable and varied to a degree, and not infrequently of a nature to weary and discourage the most enthusiastic. But I never knew Breckinridge to fail in the most insignificant task. Whatever he was ordered to do, he did thoroughly. He dignified every duty he performed.

"His professional development was remarkable, and was often the subject of comment and praise. I considered him the most capable and most competent young officer I had ever served with.

"One cold stormy night when at anchor off Staten Island, one of the boats went adrift in the gale, and as officer of the deck I had to send out a search party. It was past midnight and Breckinridge was off duty, but I knew that he was the one to find the lost launch. He appeared on deck with characteristic promptness and willingness, eager for anything that scented of unusual work, and although he did not get back for four hours, and then drenched by rain and sea, and thoroughly chilled, he reported his return with the boat as cheerfully as if he had been to a pleasure party—and to him it was a pleasure party. He knew not fear, and he loved danger and personal risk. It was his nature.

"After his final graduation, I wrote

a letter to the Navy Department
asking as a special favor that he be
detailed for the *Cushing*, knowing his
special value for such service, and on
the 15th of July, 1898, he reported
on board at Newport. From that
time, he found himself in a professional atmosphere that was most
pleasant to him. His duties as Executive Officer expanded his opportunities and presented a wide field
in which to work out new experiences. He was equal to every emergency, and during the cruise many
arose, calling from him nerve, coolness, and judgment.

"Life on a torpedo-boat is one of
such close intimacy, that it is as if
one lived constantly under the search-
light of critical inspection, and it is
an exceptional character that can
bear the scrutiny, and such was the
character of Cabell Breckinridge. It
was stainless, without fear and without reproach. He loved honor and

truth, and the soul of man. His strength was as the strength of ten, because his heart was pure. In his last hour, his death became his life, and he met his terrible fate with the courage of a hero, a smile upon his face, and his lips sealed.

"Not altogether has he died, for he still lives in the hearts of those who knew and loved him."

Thus it was his fate to be the first to give his life in the honorable effort our great liberty-loving Republic is making to put down misrule and rebellion in the Pearl of the Antilles. He knew the expedition on which he was about to sail was likely to be perilous, and just before sailing he sent his father a paper containing his last instructions. He showed in this paper many of his characteristic traits, his thoughtfulness for others, his tender affection for his family, his serene faith, and his interest in

God's service.[1] He could not foresee how soon he was to be called on for the last simple service. He expected, no doubt, that he might be called on to meet Spanish treachery and to give his life as his comrades of the *Maine* gave theirs a few days later ; or with a hero's hope he looked forward to some such scene as was enacted but a little later in the harbor of Manila when Commodore Dewey led his gallant men to glorious deeds in the storm of shot and shell that for almost the last time preached Spain's age-long gospel of chains and slavery. Not less truly than they, he gave his life for his country and the cause of human liberty. His was the love, the faith, the devotion, the service, the sacrifice. Let his also be the tribute of honor, and his life and death the inspiration of those who shall hear the story of his brief career.

[1] The Presbyterian Church at Annapolis was made his residuary legatee.

His body was brought from Havana to New York in the steamship *Seneca*, where it was met by his friends and taken to Kentucky. He was buried February 19th, in the beautiful Lexington Cemetery, in the midst of memorials of generations of his people, and just at the feet of his father's younger brother, Captain Charles Henry Breckinridge, whose life was also given to his country at the call of duty, and whose death has been a stirring influence in the heart of more than one kinsman. So with the bugle of a comrade blowing for him the last tattoo, he was laid in his long resting-place, to

" Sleep in peace with kindred ashes   .
Of the noble and the true,
Hands that never failed their country,
Hearts that never baseness knew."

A youthful soldier in his country's service, he had longer served under a higher Leader than any earthly chief.   And the loved ones who left his body there to silence and the grave, knew that he

" Gave
His body to that pleasant country's earth,
And his pure soul unto his captain Christ,
Under whose colors he had fought so long."

FINIS.

APPENDICES

I

REPORT OF LIEUT. ALBERT GLEAVES
UPON THE LOSS OF ENSIGN J. C.
BRECKINRIDGE

"U. S. T. B. *Cushing.*
HAVANA, CUBA, Feby. 12th, 1898.

SIR :

1. It is my painful duty to report that while making a passage from Key West, Florida, to this port, yesterday, February 11th, Ensign J. C. Breckinridge, U. S. Navy, fell overboard and was drowned.

2. The *Cushing* sailed from Key West at 7.10 A.M., the wind at the time being fresh from E. N. E. As soon as San Key light-house was cleared, and the course set for Havana, a moderate sea

was encountered, which continued to increase until about ten o'clock, when the vessel passed through two heavy rain-squalls. Immediately succeeding the squalls, the wind and sea moderated quickly, the wind dying away almost entirely, and hauling to E. by S. About 11.30 both wind and sea again increased, the wind going back to E. N. E. and blowing a fresh gale. The sea soon became so heavy, that when about 12.15 P.M. the coast of Cuba was sighted, it became necessary to slow the vessel from about fifteen knots to about nine knots, and head her up to the sea, which was then running from the east, or E. N. E., as near as could be judged, but it was confused and irregular. Twice green seas swept the deck.

3. About 1.30 P.M. Ensign Breckinridge, who was standing just abaft the forward smoke-stack on the starboard side, turned to come aft, when the *Cushing* suddenly gave a heavy roll to leeward, and he was thrown out against the life-lines. Extra heavy life-lines had

been stretched before leaving port, and the ridge - rope was in place. He clutched the ridge-rope, his body striking the two 3/8″ copper life-lines lower down. Both these lines parted : his feet slipped from under him on the wet deck, he lost hold of the ridge-rope, and, without a cry, went overboard.

4. I was standing by the signal mast on the starboard side and witnessed the accident, which occurred very quickly.

5. The engines were instantly stopped, two life-buoys thrown to Mr. Breckinridge, both of which fell within two or three yards of him, but were swept away by the sea.

6. The helm had been ported as soon as the accident occurred, and the lee boat cleared away and rigged out. Lookouts were stationed with orders not to lose sight for an instant of the unfortunate officer.

7. Two men, John Everetts, G. M., 1st Class, and Frank Coppage, seaman, jumped into the life-boat, but at this instant the after davit bent in its sock-

ets, thus causing the after-fall to slack and lower the stern of the boat, which the sea almost filled, and the boat swamped alongside. Coppage was hauled on board, but Everetts insisted upon remaining in the boat; the forward-fall was cut adrift, and the boat at once capsized, Everetts climbing on the keel and making an effort to paddle with his hands towards Mr. Breckinridge, who was now close aboard, floating on his back, his hands moving, but showing no other signs of consciousness. Another life-buoy was thrown which fell close to his head, and a line which fell short. At the same time he was encouraged from the *Cushing*, that he would be rescued, and also told that the life-buoy was close to him ; but he gave no signs of hearing.

8. As soon as possible, after the engines were stopped, they were started again, the port ahead, the starboard astern, but when the boat swamped with the men in it, they were again stopped, until the boat was clear of the ship, and

then started again, thus bringing Mr.
Breckinridge on the starboard bow, but
the boat was almost under the cutwater,
when the engines were again stopped,
and a line thrown to Everetts, who was
hauled on board. It was at this time
that the third life-buoy was thrown to
Mr. Breckinridge. The *Cushing* continued to turn head to sea by means of
helm and engines, and laid within thirty
feet of Mr. Breckinridge. Just before
we reached him a tremendous breaking
sea swept over him, and when it passed
he was floating face down, his face
under the water.

John Everetts, with a heavy line in
his hand, dived from the turtle-back,
seized Mr. Breckinridge and secured
the line around his body. At this time
Daniel Atkins, ship's cook, jumped
overboard to assist Everetts. It was
with great difficulty that Mr. Breckinridge, Everetts and Atkins were gotten
aboard.

9. From the time that Mr. Breckinridge fell overboard until the men were

all picked up, cannot be accurately
stated, but it was probably not longer
than fifteen minutes.

10. Everything that was possible to
be done to resuscitate Mr. Breckinridge
was practiced from the time he was
picked up until 5 P.M., without a moment's interruption.

When Mr. Breckinridge fell overboard
he had on his rain coat and rubber
boots ; the latter he got off.

11. After the accident the *Cushing*
steamed slowly to the eastward for
nearly an hour, in order to make the
work of resuscitation as comfortable as
possible.

12. At 2.30 P.M., fires having been
lighted in the after boiler, and the sea
having somewhat moderated, the vessel
was headed to the westward under all
possible steam, and arrived off Morro
Castle at 3 P.M.

13. Assistance from the U. S. S.
Maine was immediately obtained, and
shortly afterwards assistance from shore,
and as stated above, the effort to restore
life was not abandoned until 5 P.M.

14. By the death of Ensign Breckinridge, the service loses a young officer of rare merit and exceptional ability ; one who gave every promise of a useful and brilliant career.

15. The gallant conduct of John Everetts and Daniel Atkins deserves special commendation and recognition.

Very respectfully,

(sig.) ALBERT GLEAVES,

Lieutenant U. S. Navy, Commanding *Cushing*.

Captain Charles D. Sigsbee, U. S. Navy, Commanding U. S. S. *Maine*, and Senior Officer Present."

II

FUNERAL SERMON BY REV. WALLACE
RADCLIFFE, D.D., AT LEXINGTON,
KENTUCKY, FEBRUARY 19, 1898,
IN MEMORY OF ENSIGN J. C. BRECK-
INRIDGE

THE day even in its natural decline
is prophetic. Its sentiment is one
of sadness and fear. The usual twilight
brings the retrospect of incompleteness,
and often the sad and pathetic forebod-
ing. It is therefore more impressive
when we realize the prophecy of Amos,
" I will cause the sun to go down at
noon, and will darken the earth in the
clear day." The bereavement of to-day

is in the darkness and pathos of a noon-day eclipse. This life, to the common apprehension, had not lived out half its days. In its death the sun has gone down at noon. Of an honored name, of distinguished lineage, with natural and winning gifts of body, mind, and char-acter, and in the recent completion of his preparatory work, we all recognized its opportunity and laudable ambition of higher usefulness, enduring activity and large renown. But in the very moment, unexpectedly, there comes extinguish-ment, darkness, and the end. It all seems a mistake, a failure, a disaster. Naturally, loved ones wait in despair, refusing to be comforted. But when the sun goes down off this world it rises on other and brighter worlds. Its mis-sion is to richer experiences and more beneficent results. The sun itself is not lost. Light is not destroyed. If this ends all, then life is a failure. If we enter into the opportunities, exhilara-tions, and ambitions of the present ex-istence only to have them snatched away

in the moment of realization, then this
life is not worth living.

But this life is not all. The sun that
here goes down rises on other worlds.
Out of the present life-work, however
short, come character, and preparation,
and experiences for other worlds and
more enduring service. It is not for us
to interpret the individual and isolated
affliction. This we know, that every experience will have its interpretation and
this interpretation will be love, and the
end will be life. "What I do thou
knowest not now, but thou shalt know
hereafter." We must guard ourselves
against the subtlety of selfish sorrow.
Around all individual experiences swings
the circle of the only infinite wisdom. We
are to abide in the assurance of wisdom
beyond our own, and of intent beyond
the limitations of our momentary vision.
We must remember and assume the
right standpoint. The unbeliever judges
the character of God by the trying dispensation. The believer judges the trying dispensation by the character of God.

Be sure there is no accident, no chance,
no fate. The finger of God has traced
every step. It is not for us to know the
end from the beginning. All things
minister to us, and for us, whilst we look
at the unseen and eternal things. Even
Jesus prayed that if it were possible, the
cup might pass from him ; but mark the
submission and perfectness of his faith :
" Not my will, but Thine." Then out
of that cup came not only bitterness
but strength, conquest, ascension, gifts
and eternal life. The cup of bitterness
had intimate association with the cross.
But to him who drinks it with Christ's
lips it has just as intimate association
with the beauty of resurrection and the
glory of ascension.

None of us knows what God is doing
with us. Always He is wise. Always
He is fatherly. Always, if we will, He
is ordaining grace and unexpected and
enlarging blessing. You will remember
the sore and reproachful lamentation
of Jacob : " Joseph is not ; Simeon
is not, and ye will take Benjamin

away.　All these things are against me."

And yet all these things were not against him.　All these things were for him though he knew it not.　If God had responded to the immediate desire of Jacob, Joseph and Simeon and Benjamin would have been close to Jacob's vision, but in the answer to Jacob's selfishness and limitations, it had been worse for Jacob and for humanity.　The things that were against Jacob were the best things for him, for his race and for the world.　The trend of history, the dispensation of grace, the highest interests of humanity were changed because for a little while things seemed to be against him and his house.

I know not the meaning of this dispensation, but I am sure that though Joseph be not, even these things are for you and will continue to be for you whilst you look not at the things which are seen and temporal.

That was a beautiful expression when of olden time it was often said of the departed that "he was gathered unto his people." It is a beautiful and fit thing that our brother should find his resting-place here where his family name has been so honored, and where his own people for the generations have lain waiting for the resurrection. Here are his people whose patriotism, sterling character, and religious service have given influence and honor to the family name. It is right and beautiful that he should lie resting in these beautiful hills, waiting to rise with his own to the promised recognition and reward. But in a higher and truer sense, even had he lain in the depths of the sea, he is gathered unto his people. His own kinfolk, his people, are those to whom his spirit has gone, and with whom he already finds congenial companionship and service. When a soul believes in Jesus Christ ; when the human hand has grasped that divine hand, and the human heart that divine heart, there flows forth that one eternal life, pulsating and vivifying, which makes us forever and forever of

the people of God. They are distinctly
our people. We are their kin. Heaven
is our home. God is our Father.

It is right on this occasion that we be
reminded of his profession of faith in
Jesus Christ. Consistently, honestly,
beautifully, he believed God, and it was
counted to him for righteousness. He
recognized the stormy sea on which his
boat was struggling ; he knew the peril
and the weakness of earthly promise.
His faith grasped a life-line that never
yet has broken—that never can break,
—whose strands were made in Heaven,
and bear within them the Almighti-
ness of God. The moment of his weakness was the moment of Almighty
strength. His has been rescue into
calm and eternal safety. He has joined
his kinfolk and has place and joy in
the house not made with hands. A life
that was beautiful, a character that was
honest, an aim that was heroic, a work
that was complete, a service that was
faithful, he proved himself the good son
and brother, the honest friend, the brave

man. As we leave him tenderly among his own people, assured of his rest and reward, we hear, as of old, the loving words of the Master, " Thy friend, thy son, thy brother, shall rise again."

www.ingramcontent.com/pod-product-compliance
Lightning Source LLC
Chambersburg PA
CBHW022140020726
47496CB00008B/2487